I Love You Dino-Mummy

Mark Sperring

Illustrated by Sam Lloyd

BLOOMSBURY
LONDON OXFORD NEW YORK NEW DELHI SYDNEY

Do you know a secret?
I'm sure you dino-do!

It's something rather special
about a certain "you know who!"

From the moment that you wake up
she's a sing-song superstar,
singing out,

"Good Morning!"

At breakfast, she's amazing —
watch the toast fly through the air!

She's a
dino-conjure-upper...

As if that wasn't
fab enough,

of course there's
dino-more . . .

She's a kiss-it-better doctor
when she hears your dino-roar.

She's the star of the high wire —

Gasp!

hanging washing on the line.

And the bravest dino-trooper...
fighting

dust

and grease

and grime.

Much later after dino-lunch,

5, 4, 3, 2, 1!

She can be your rocket launcher.
HURRAH! What dino-fun!

And when it's time for dress-up –

can you believe your eyes?

At bath time she's a GENIUS!
Please clap your claws together!

In fact, there is no secret.
It's as clear as dino-day,
from the moment
that you wake up . . .

well, she's great in

So when dino-bedtime comes around,
and you're tucked up oh sooo snuggly,
there's only one thing left to say...

For Dino-Mummies everywhere ~ MS

For my sisters Becky and Jess, and all the
other dino-mummies out there ~ SL

Bloomsbury Publishing, London, Oxford, New York, New Delhi and Sydney
First published in Great Britain in 2014 by Bloomsbury Publishing Plc

50 Bedford Square, London WC1B 3DP
This padded hardback edition first published in 2018

www.bloomsbury.com

BLOOMSBURY is a registered trademark of Bloomsbury Publishing Plc

Text copyright © Mark Sperring 2014
Illustrations copyright © Sam Lloyd 2014

The moral rights of the author and illustrator have been asserted

A CIP catalogue record of this book is available from the British Library

ISBN 978 1 4088 9343 2

All papers used by Bloomsbury Publishing are natural, recyclable products made
from wood grown in well managed forests. The manufacturing processes
conform to the environmental regulations of the country of origin

Printed in China by Leo Paper Products, Heshan, Guangdong
1 3 5 7 9 10 8 6 4 2